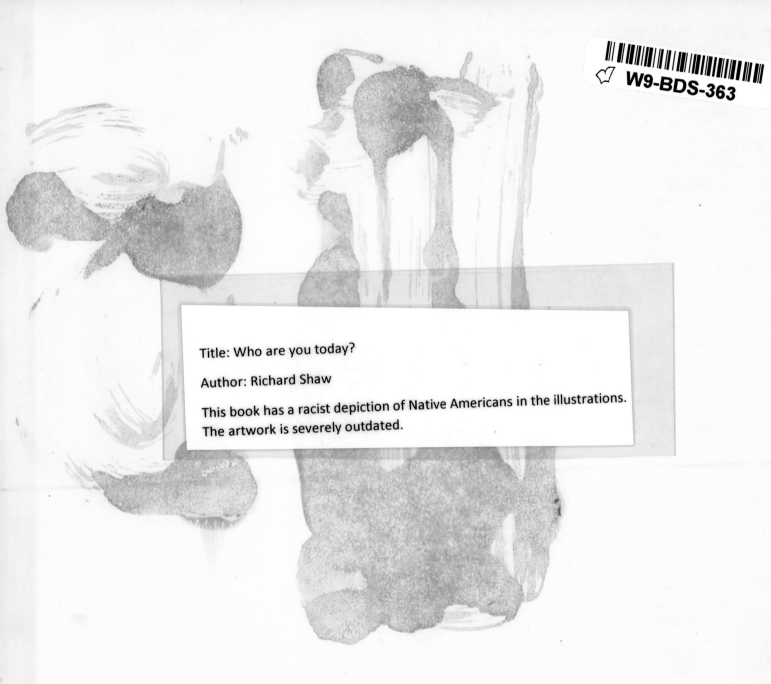

Title: Who are you today?

Author: Richard Shaw

This book has a racist depiction of Native Americans in the illustrations. The artwork is severely outdated.

Who Are You Today?

Who

Are You Today?

by **RICHARD SHAW**

illustrated by KURT WERTH

Frederick Warne and Company, Inc. *New York and London*

For Janet

When Jeff's mother heard
A knock at the door,
She peeped out the window,
And there as before
A stranger stood,
For every day
A stranger called
While Jeff was at play:

Sometimes a Martian,
Or an Indian brave,
And Jeff's mother knew
Just how to behave
With cowboys, firemen
And acrobats—
She knew who they were
By their different hats.
She opened the door,
In her usual way,
And said to the stranger,
"Who are you today?

You can't be the milkman,
You can't be a knight,
And you can't be a sailor,
Your hat isn't white;
You might be a farmer,
If your hat were straw,
Or a carpenter,
But you have no saw.
I do not know
From the way you dress,
Or your funny old hat,
I can't even guess
Who you are today.

Won't you please come in,
And tell me your story
And where you've been?"
"I thought you'd know,"
Said Jeff with a frown,
"I'm Poco-Loco,
The famous clown."
Jeff's mother gasped,
"The Great Poco-Loco!
Tell me your story,
While I make you some cocoa."

The Clown's Story
I'm the funniest clown
In the world because I
Make noises so loud
People think I'm a crowd.
I can wiggle my ears,
My hands are all dirty,
My shoes are untied,
And I leave things outside.

I turn on the hose,
My hair is all mussed,
My shirt tails hang out,
And I giggle and shout.
That's why everyone laughs
At the Great Poco-Loco;
Now you've heard my story,
And I want my cocoa.

On Saturday morning,
As the clock struck ten,
The doorbell rang,
And once again
A stranger was there,
All ragged and worn,
His jacket was ripped,
And his pants were torn.
There were holes in his hat,
There were holes in his sweater,
There were holes in his shoes,
And he held out a letter,
And the letter said:
"Dear Jeff's Mom,
Take care of this orphan,
His name is Tom."

"Won't you please come in,"
Jeff's mother said,
And tell me your story
While I bake corn bread?"

The Orphan's Story

Orphans like me stay up very late,
Watching TV till a quarter past eight.
No one's around to put them to bed,
So they dawdle along and play Moon Man instead.
They leave dirty clothes in a heap on the floor;
They eat peanut butter and then eat some more;
They never wear rubbers, they play in the rain,
They ask the same questions again and again;
And nobody says, "Not now, dear," or "We'll see,"
Or "It all depends on what the weather will be."

Orphans never take naps, they never eat liver;
They don't put on sweaters whenever they shiver;
They track mud in the house, they wrinkle the rugs;
They play with the phone and are friendly with bugs.
They live with lost kittens and stray puppies who
Follow them home, 'cause they're lonely too.
"So, being an orphan," Jeff's mother said,
"Is really great fun. Now, have some corn bread."
"The trouble with orphans," Jeff said as he ate,
"Is they get kind of scared at a quarter past eight."

When Jeff's mother heard
A knocking one night,
She went to the door
All ready to invite
Whoever was there
To come in for a chat,
And munch shortbread,

And hang up his hat;
But all she could see
On the porch in the dark,
Was part of a sheet
With her laundry mark.
Then she heard a weird voice,
From behind a post
Say, "You can't see me,
'Cause I am a ghost."
"Come on in, spook,
And have a seat,
But be very careful
Not to tear my sheet."

The weird voice said,
"You must not look
While I pass through the walls
To the breakfast nook."
She closed her eyes
And heard awful groans,
Then from under the table
Came terrible moans.
Then the ghost's voice said,
In a spooky way,
"Now I'll tell you how
I got this way."

The Spook's Story
My parents got angry
At something I said,
Last night at the table,
And they sent me to bed.

In my bed! In my room!
Not wandering about!
In pajamas! Teeth brushed!
Tucked in! Lights out!
I wasn't sleepy,
So I built a big thing
Out of junk I'd collected,
And some wire and some string,
And while I was building,
I decided I ought
To live somewhere else.
Yes, that's what I thought!
"They don't want me around!
I don't have to stay!"

I said to myself,
"So I'll just run away.
They'll be awful sorry.
They'll hunt and they'll call.
They'll miss *me* a lot.
I won't miss *them* at all.
No, I have a plan
That's better than that—
I'll put on my old
Invisible hat,
And watch Mother cry,
And hear Daddy say,
How lonely they are
Since I went away."

Jeff's mother gasped,
"Oh, we missed you so!
We felt so upset,
'Cause we didn't know
You were invisible—
Asleep in your bed—
And we searched everywhere,
In the cellar and shed.
Please, take off your hat,
So we'll know where you are,
And have some shortbread
From the big cookie jar."
"Spooks get awful hungry,
And quite lonely too,"
Said Jeff as he munched,
"And there's not much to do.
They don't pull wagons,
Or play with a cat,
So I think I'll take off
My invisible hat."

But strangers still called
At the house as before—
Once every day
Jeff knocked at the door—
Once as a robot,
Twice as a knight,
And three or four times
As a chef dressed in white.
And every day,
He wore a new hat,
And nibbled at something,
And had a nice chat,
Till on a cold morning,
One day in the fall,
Jeff knocked at the door
With no hat on at all.

He said to his mother,
Very seriously,
"Mom, starting today,
I think I'll be ME."